Hello, friends! Are you ready to leap into some pawsitively amazing adventures? Then let's join Max, a fluffy and brave dog who's always finding himself in extraordinary situations!

From finding a hidden world under the city to having fun with alien pups in a faraway galaxy, each story will take you to a fantastic new world full of fun, surprises, and friendship.
Get ready for a tail-wagging good time and let your imagination soar with Max's incredible adventures!

THIS BOOK BELONGS TO:

NAME _____.

AGE _____.

THE ADVENTURES OF MAX

Contents

The Day Max Flew

The sun shone brightly over Pineville Park, casting a golden glow over the playground, the duck pond, and the vast green fields that spread out as far as the eye could see. Families gathered to enjoy picnics, children chased after their runaway soccer balls, and the scent of grilled burgers wafted through the air.

Sally, Ben, and Max arrived at the park with a picnic basket in tow and a bright red frisbee specially bought for Max. After settling down on a comfy blanket, Ben decided it was the perfect time to play fetch with Max.

"Ready, Max?" Ben called out, waving the frisbee to catch the little Shih Tzu's attention.
Max barked in excitement, his tail wagging furiously, his eyes fixated on the frisbee.

With a strong throw, Ben sent the frisbee soaring into the air. But just as the frisbee caught the wind, an unexpected gust swept through the park. The frisbee went higher and higher, and Max, jumped to catch it.

To everyone's astonishment, instead of coming back down, Max kept going up! The wind had caught the loose fabric of his little harness, and he began to float upwards like a furry balloon.
"Max!" Sally shouted in disbelief.
Ben gasped. "Hold on, buddy!"

Families around the park stopped to point and stare. A floating dog was not something you saw every day! Some kids cheered, thinking it was a fun trick, while others looked worriedly at the sky.

Max, for his part, seemed a bit confused but not particularly frightened. He managed to grab onto the frisbee with his mouth, wagging his tail as he hovered over the park.

Sally tried to think quickly. "Ben, we need something to pull him down—a net or a long rope!"

Ben spotted a kite vendor nearby. "The kites! We can use the strings!" he exclaimed.

They rushed to the vendor, quickly explaining the situation. With the help of other park-goers, they attached multiple kite strings together, creating a long makeshift rope. Ben tied a soft toy to one end to catch Max's attention.

"Here, boy! Come get the toy!" Ben shouted, swinging the toy in the air.

Max, noticing the toy below, started paddling his paws as if he could swim down. Slowly but surely, the combination of Max's effort and the pulling from below brought the floating Shih Tzu closer to the ground.

With one final pull, Max was safely back on solid ground. The park erupted in applause. Max, ever the showman, took a playful bow, still holding onto his frisbee.

Sally hugged Max tightly. "You gave us quite a scare there, buddy!"

Ben laughed, ruffling Max's fur. "Guess we found a new way for you to fetch, eh?"

Underground Adventures

The next weekend, with the floating incident still fresh in their minds, the family decided to go on a different kind of adventure. They planned a trip to the Pineville Caves – a popular tourist spot known for its beautiful underground stalactites and stalagmites.

After a short drive, they arrived at the entrance to the caves. Sally read aloud from the guidebook, "Legend says these caves were once the hideouts of pirates and might still hold buried treasures." Ben's eyes sparkled at the thought, and even Max seemed intrigued, his ears perking up.

As they made their way deeper into the caves, the trio followed a well-lit path, marveling at the sparkling crystals overhead and the echoing drips of water. Max was particularly intrigued by the echoes, occasionally barking just to hear the sound bounce back at him.

After some time, they reached an area that was cordoned off with a sign that read, "Do Not Enter - Unexplored Territory." Ben peered beyond the ropes, curiosity piqued. "I wonder what's on the other side," he whispered.

Suddenly, Max's sharp ears picked up a faint sound. It was a distant jingling noise, like the sound of coins clinking together. Without warning, the little Shih Tzu ducked under the rope and bolted into the unexplored section.

"Max!" Sally and Ben exclaimed in unison, dashing after him.
The path here was narrower, and the ceiling hung lower. They could barely see, but the soft glow of Sally's flashlight revealed paw prints in the damp soil. They followed the trail, which led them to a large open chamber.

In the center of the chamber stood an old wooden chest, half-buried in the ground, with a few coins scattered around. The jingling sound was louder now – caused by water droplets falling on the metal coins.

Max sat beside the chest, wagging his tail, proud of his discovery. Ben knelt beside the chest, brushing off the dirt. "It's a real treasure chest!" he exclaimed.

Sally, though, was more cautious. "We should inform the cave authorities about this. It could be a part of Pineville's history."

With Max leading the way, the trio made their way back to the main path and quickly informed the cave guides about their find. The discovery was indeed significant, and the chest was believed to be a remnant from the days when pirates roamed the seas.

As a token of appreciation, the Pineville Caves management rewarded Max with a year's supply of his favorite treats and a special tag that read "Pineville's Treasure Hunter."

The family left the caves with their hearts full of excitement and pride. Max, with his nose high in the air and his new tag jingling, strutted around, clearly enjoying his new status as a hero.

Max's Dreamland Adventure

In the warmth of a starry night, Max fell into a deep, peaceful slumber. His little paws twitched as he dreamed, transported to a fantastical world unlike any other.

As he opened his eyes, Max found himself in a realm filled with hues of purples, pinks, and golds. The trees whispered secrets, and the flowers gently hummed lullabies. In this magical world, Max was the king! His crown was a dazzling array of golden leaves, and his robe was woven with the soft hues of countless sunsets.

He roamed his kingdom, barking in delight at the dancing butterflies and the rivers that giggled as they flowed. But soon, Max realized that being a king was more than just frolic and fun.

His subjects, a myriad of talking animals, came to him with their concerns. Squirrels needed help with nut storage, rabbits sought assistance in burrow building, and the singing birds wished for new songs to sing.

Max, though overwhelmed, listened attentively to each one. His heart swelled with compassion as he tried to solve their problems, realizing that ruling was not just about wearing a crown, but about caring, understanding and responsibility.

In his royal court, under a sky lit with fireflies, Max held a grand meeting. The creatures of his dreamland gathered, their eyes filled with hope and respect. With a soft but firm bark, Max shared his ideas, his wisdom bringing harmony and happiness to his magical realm.

He helped the squirrels design a brilliant nut-storage system using the river's gentle flow. For the rabbits, he organized a team of sturdy beavers to construct robust and cozy burrows. And for the birds, he called upon the winds to carry melodies from distant lands, bringing fresh songs to their wings.

As the dreamland blossomed in unity and joy, Max felt a profound warmth in his heart, the love of his subjects enveloping him in a tender embrace. Yet, amidst the celebrations, a soft, familiar call echoed, reaching the depths of his dream.

"Max! Wake up, sweet boy!"
As the magical world gently faded, Max woke to the loving faces of Sally and Ben, their smiles bathed in the morning light.

He wagged his tail, his dream leaving whispers of warmth in his heart, whispers that echoed throughout his days, filling them with the gentle hues of kindness, understanding, and boundless love.

The Alien Dog Park

One clear night, while the crickets chirped and the moon painted silver paths on the garden paths, Max was in the backyard chasing fireflies. Their lights blinked on and off, leading him on a merry dance.

Suddenly, the night grew quiet. The fireflies dispersed as a strange humming filled the air. Max's ears perked up, and his fluffy tail paused in mid-wag. Above, a swirling vortex of colors illuminated the sky. It was a UFO, its lights bright and entrancing.

Before Max could bark, a beam of light gently lifted him from the ground, carrying him into the spacecraft.

Inside, Max found himself in a place beyond his wildest doggy dreams - an intergalactic dog park! The park was filled with open spaces, swirling in hues of neon blues and vibrant greens, under a shimmering cosmic canopy.

Alien pups of all shapes, sizes and colors were happily playing. Some had multiple tails, others had glowing fur, and a few even floated in mid-air.

Max's initial apprehension transformed into curiosity. An alien pup with luminescent wings flew up to him, barking in a funny, musical tone.

Max barked back, and soon they were chasing each other, leaping over small asteroids and running on rainbow bridges that materialized in the air.

Max learned new games that he had never imagined. He played fetch with a ball that changed shape and color, and tug-of-war with a sentient rope that playfully tugged back. He sipped on water that floated in bubbles and munched on treats that gently floated down from a cloud of stars.

In this marvelous cosmic playground, Max made friends with alien pups from galaxies far and wide.

They shared stories of their planets, painting images in the stardust that sparkled around them. Max showed them his favorite tricks, earning cheers and joyful barks from his new friends.

After a delightful time, the winged pup nudged Max gently, leading him back to the beam of light. Max barked his goodbyes, his heart full of the extraordinary adventure and the friends he made.

As the UFO gently set Max back in his backyard, the alien pups waved their tails from the spaceship window, their goodbyes twinkling like stars. Max wagged his tail back as the UFO disappeared into the cosmos, its lights fading into the vast tapestry of the universe.

Back on Earth, Max looked up at the stars, his bark a soft echo in the quiet night, sending a warm hello to the friends beyond, waiting for the day they would meet again in the cosmic dance of interstellar barks and tail wags.

Max and the Lighthouse Mystery

The sun painted the sky with shades of pink and orange as Sally, Ben, and Max arrived in a quaint seaside town. The town was abuzz with stories of a haunted lighthouse, casting a long, mysterious shadow over the rocky shore. Intrigued and excited, the family decided to explore the lighthouse and find out the truth.

As they strolled by the beach, the lighthouse stood tall and majestic, its walls weathered by the salt and storms of countless years. The town's folks had spoken of eerie lights, strange noises, and sudden chills, turning the once bustling tourist spot into a place whispered about in hushed tones.

Sally and Ben, a bit hesitant, decided to tour the town while Max, brave and curious, made his way towards the lighthouse. The large, round structure loomed ahead, its door creaking softly in the sea breeze.

Max slipped inside and was met by a spiral staircase winding up to the top. With a slight tremble in his paws, he ascended the steps. He heard whispers of long-lost sailors and felt the cool brush of unseen hands. Steadily, Max continued, his nose wiggling, catching scents of the past.

Reaching the top, Max was greeted by a breathtaking view of the sea, shimmering under the setting sun. In the center of the room, the large light of the lighthouse cast its glow far and wide.

Amidst the beauty, Max noticed a shadow, fragile and faded. It was the spirit of the old lighthouse keeper, his ethereal form gently tending to the light that had guided countless ships safely to the shore.

The ghost, noticing Max, smiled warmly, his form a soft glimmer. In the hushed whispers of the wind, Max heard the tales of the keeper, his love for the lighthouse, and his undying dedication to the safety of the sailors at sea.

The keeper's spirit had lingered to ensure the light never went out, his presence turning into tales of hauntings. Max, with a soft wag of his tail, acknowledged the keeper's noble mission, offering a gentle bark of thanks.

As Max made his way back to rejoin Sally and Ben, the lighthouse keeper's spirit waved a fond farewell, his form dissolving into a warm, serene light, finally at peace, knowing his beloved lighthouse would continue to stand tall and proud, a beacon of safety in the vast embrace of the sea.

Back with Sally and Ben, Max watched the lighthouse from a distance, its light a steady pulse against the dusk sky, a sentinel of stories, whispers, and timeless dedication, guarding the mysteries of the sea, under the watchful gaze of the stars above.

Museum Mischief

The museum stood tall and grand, its pillars like giant sentinels guarding the treasures of the past. Sally, Ben, and Max entered its vast halls, where echoes of ancient times whispered through the air.

As they wandered through the various exhibits, from dinosaur bones stretched towards the ceilings to intricate paintings adorning the walls, Max's little nose quivered, sniffing out centuries of history. The trio eventually reached the Egyptian exhibit, where a life-sized replica of a pharaoh's tomb lay.

Max's paws padded softly on the cold floor as he explored, his curiosity piqued by the strange hieroglyphs and artifacts.

A mummy's sarcophagus rested in the center of the room, half-open to display its ancient occupant to the modern world.

In the excitement of exploration, Max's wagging tail accidentally brushed against a small, hidden lever on the sarcophagus. With a silent shudder, the ancient coffin creaked open entirely. Max's ears perked up and his fur stood on end as he watched the mummy slowly sit up, dust and ancient wrappings unfurling.

Sally and Ben, absorbed in examining a nearby exhibit, missed the magical moment that brought the mummy to life. The mummy, however, was not menacing or menacingly moody. With playful ancient eyes, it peered at Max, throwing a time-worn object on the floor towards him. Max, despite his initial fear, couldn't resist his natural instincts. He fetched the object – an ancient Egyptian toy – and brought it back to the mummy.

Thus began a playful game of fetch through the hallowed halls of the museum, the mummy's ancient laughter mingling with Max's joyful barks. They dashed past grand statues and delicate vases, a lively spectacle against the backdrop of silent history.

Finally, noticing the silence, Sally and Ben turned around to witness the unbelievable scene. Their gasps of surprise echoed through the chamber as they saw Max and the mummy in the midst of their playful prance.

Realizing its time was limited, the mummy led Max back to its resting place. With a gentle pat, it bid goodbye to its furry friend, lying back in the sarcophagus. Max, understanding the unspoken words, nudged the lever, closing the ancient coffin with a soft thud.

As they left the museum, the adventure tucked in their hearts, Max gave one last glance to the Egyptian exhibit, his tail wagging gently. The secret of the playful pharaoh would be safe with him, a tale whispered only in the winds of the past and the soft woof of a small, adventurous dog.

The Circus Spectacle

One sunny afternoon, the small town was abuzz with excitement. A colorful circus had rolled in, filling the air with the scent of popcorn and the sound of merry laughter. Sally, Ben, and Max decided to join the fun, eager to see the acrobats, clowns, and exotic animals.

As they arrived at the bustling circus grounds, a vibrant parade of performers welcomed them.

Acrobats tumbled, clowns juggled, and exotic animals showcased their grandeur. Amid the marvel and mirth, Max's small, fluffy form caught the eye of a frazzled circus manager.

In a whirlwind of confusion, the manager mistook Max for a famous circus dog that had gone missing. "There you are, Fuzzball the Fantastic!" he exclaimed, scooping Max up in his arms and rushing towards the big top. Despite his barks of protest, Max found himself in a dressing room filled with glittering costumes and colorful props.

With a small, snug costume, Max was transformed into "Fuzzball the Fantastic", ready for the grand performance. Under the big top, a sea of eager faces awaited the spectacle. Max peered out from the backstage, his eyes wide with anticipation and nervousness.

Sally and Ben, who had been searching frantically for Max, took their seats, unaware that their beloved pooch was the upcoming star. The circus music swelled, and the spotlight shined on Max as he was announced as "the most extraordinary dog under the stars!"

With a gentle nudge from the kind-hearted trapeze artists, Max stepped onto the center stage, his tiny paws padding on the soft sawdust. He gazed at the cheering crowd and recognized the familiar faces of Sally and Ben, their eyes filled with surprise and delight.

Encouraged by their presence, Max embraced the unexpected adventure. He danced, leaped through hoops, and balanced on a giant ball, earning roars of applause from the amazed audience.

His final trick, a high-flying leap from a mini cannon, sent him soaring through a ring of tiny stars, landing perfectly in a net adorned with glitter.

The crowd erupted in cheers and claps as Max took a bow, the circus lights shimmering on his little costume. Sally and Ben rushed to the stage, hugging their brave, talented dog, their laughter mingling with the joyful circus music.

After clearing the confusion and sharing laughs with the circus crew, Max, Sally, and Ben said their goodbyes, Max's tail wagging in the cool evening breeze. As they walked away from the colorful tents, the stars above echoed the sparkle of their unforgettable circus adventure, Max's little barks a merry tune in the symphony of the night.

Island of the Cat King

One sunny afternoon, as Max played by the seaside, a playful wave swept him off his paws and into a bobbing boat that broke free from its anchor. Max's heart thudded against his furry chest as the boat was carried by the whimsical winds across the endless expanse of the ocean.

The sun dipped below the horizon, painting the sky with hues of pink and orange before plunging the world into star-studded darkness.

When the dawn broke, the boat softly thudded against a sandy shore. Max leaped out, shaking the sea spray off his coat. Before him lay an island with lush forests, majestic waterfalls, and colorful flowers blooming in abundance. However, the enchanting beauty held a peculiar secret.

Max noticed countless cats of all shapes and sizes, lazily stretched out under the sun, playfully chasing butterflies, and agilely climbing trees. The cats' eyes followed Max with a mix of curiosity and amusement as he trotted through the island, searching for a way back home.

At the heart of the island, upon a velvet throne under a silken canopy, sat a majestic cat with glossy, white fur and golden eyes that shimmered like jewels. Max approached with tentative steps.

"Who dares enter the realm of King Whiskers?" boomed the regal voice of the majestic feline.

With a polite bow, Max introduced himself and narrated his unintended journey to the island. King Whiskers, though proud, was a cat of compassion. He offered Max a deal. If Max could complete three tasks on the island, the King would guide him back home.

The tasks were not easy. Max had to climb a towering tree to retrieve a jeweled necklace, outwit a crafty cat in a game of riddles, and navigate through a maze filled with tantalizing scents and distractions. With each challenge, Max discovered the grace, agility, and cleverness of the feline inhabitants, who moved with a silent, elegant confidence through their island realm.

Completing the tasks with a newfound respect for his feline counterparts, Max stood again before King Whiskers, panting but proud. True to his word, King Whiskers ordered the swiftest cats to guide Max to a hidden path that led to the mainland.

As Max bade goodbye to the Island of the Cat King, he glanced back at the paradise where cats reigned supreme, a smile on his snout and a treasure trove of tales wagging along with his tail. The adventure echoed in the gentle sea waves, whispering the stories of an island where cats ruled, and dogs, albeit temporarily, drooled!

MARVELOUS DOG TREATS

Would you like to some special treats for Max? With the help of an adult, you can make some tasty treats for your dog and their friends to enjoy!
You'll just need some cookie cutters, and a few simple ingredients.

PLEASE REMEMBER TO ALWAYS CHECK WITH AN ADULT BEFORE USING THE OVEN AND MAKE SURE THAT THE INGREDIENTS ARE SAFE FOR YOUR DOG.

Ingredients

- 1 1/4 cup of Oat Flour (Make your own by blending old fashioned oats in a food processor)
- 1/4 cup of Unsweetened Applesauce
- 2 tbsp of Peanut Butter (No Xylitol as it is toxic to dogs. Aim for single ingredient peanut butter)
- 3/4 cup of mashed Purple or Orange Sweet Potato

1. Preheat oven to 350 F
2. Peel, slice, and boil your orange OR purple sweet potato in water for 15 minutes. Mash with a fork and set aside.
3. Combine all ingredients in a bowl and thoroughly combine. Refrigerate the dough for 10-15 minutes if you're using cookie cutters. This will make it much easier to roll out and cut into shapes.
4. Roll out dough to 1/4 inch thickness and use your cookie cutters to cut out shapes. Lay shapes on a parchment lined baking sheets. These do not spread while baking, so you can place them close together.
5. Bake for 22-25 minutes. Treats will be firm and slightly browned on the bottom. Allow to fully cool before serving.

Leave to cool completely.

Baking time will vary depending on the size and thickness of the treats. Serving size will also vary depending on the shapes and cookie cutters used.

THE END

Printed in Great Britain
by Amazon